Warriors

#5

LOST IN SPACE™

THE NEW JOURNEYS

Warriors

J. J. GARDNER

SCHOLASTIC INC.
New York Toronto London Auckland Sydney

ISBN 0-590-18942-5

12 11 10 9 8 7 6 5 4 3 2 1   9/9 0 1 2 3/0

Printed in the U.S.A.

First Scholastic printing, January 1999

Warriors

1
Fuel Stop

"Life in space is dull, Will. It's one percent adventure and ninety-nine percent computer maintenance."

Ten-year-old Will Robinson remembered Dr. Smith's words as he pressed a sequence of entries into the Robotics station diagnostic program and waited. It would take a few minutes for the program to boot up, then another few minutes for the systems maintenance check to begin running. Then there would be the hours of waiting.

Catching a glimpse of himself in the reflection of the station's monitor, Will saw two tired eyes under his short shock of light brown hair. Running a diagnostic on the Robotics station was boring, thought Will. *Very* boring. First there were the land probes. Each one had to be checked from the inside out. Then there were the orbital probes and their respective launch chambers. Finally, there were the on-board robots: the complex collection of moving armatures and cams that couldn't be seen. They were deep inside the machinery of the *Jupiter 2* spaceship, the huge vehicle that carried Will and his family through unmapped outer space as they searched for a way back home, to Earth. These internal "mini-robots" helped the *Jupiter 2* operate smoothly. There were nearly a thousand of them and each one had to have a computer check done individually.

Of course, it wouldn't be so bad if the *Jupiter 2* was still in space. In space, there was often so little to do that running systems checks could be a distraction from the endless emptiness of the unfamiliar cosmos.

But the *Jupiter 2* wasn't in space now. Months ago Will's father had scheduled this fuel regeneration stop. As soon as a suitable planet was found, one that had safe oxygen to breath and enough subterranean deutronium to mine, Professor Robinson and Major West took the *Jupiter* in for a landing.

Fuel mining could take days or weeks. For Will's dad it was the perfect time to order a complete departmental rundown, the kind that can only be done when most of the ship's systems were not in use. That meant that while he and Major West mined for deutronium, everyone was responsible for checking their particular station from top to bottom.

As Will heard the diagnostic program start up, his mind began to wander. What kind of planet were they on? What colors were the lakes and oceans? What was the sand made of? Were there any intelligent aliens living here?

That last question was probably already answered, Will realized, as he set the diagnostic program to automatically begin its analysis of the *Jupiter 2*'s various probes and robots. If there were any intelligent alien life forms on the planet, his mom would have detected them at the life science station before they landed. That was one of his father's rules when searching for a possible refueling site: the planet should be uninhabited. They had encountered too many hostile aliens on their travels so far to risk contact. It was better to land someplace where the Robinsons would not be confused with hostile invaders.

But, still, Will wished he could be out exploring the new planet instead of working inside the spaceship. From the first moment they landed he had been struck by the strange new world.

"WOW!" he had exclaimed after unstrapping himself from his landing seat and running to the main viewport of the *Jupiter 2* just after landing. "Look at the size of those plants!"

"Those buttercups are as big as houses!" said his fourteen-year-old sister Penny. Her dark-painted lips opened with awe as she joined her brother at the wide window. "Freaky."

"I'd hate to see the size of the bees that pollinate them," remarked Dr. Smith when he saw the view. His dark, deep-set eyes always belied a fear for the worst. "They could be monstrous!"

"There are no bees on this planet, monstrous or otherwise," said Will's mother, Dr. Maureen Robinson, as she joined the others at the viewport. Her sharp, angular features presented the very picture of a scientist's confidence. "My life sciences scan showed only plant life indigenous to this planet."

"A new planet, a new danger," Dr. Smith replied with an ominous tone. "If not bees, I'm sure there's some evil alien out there to be afraid of."

"It takes one to know one," quipped Major West, who was just finishing locking down the ship's landing engines.

"I take that as a compliment, Major," replied Dr. Smith defiantly.

"Environmental conditions are confirmed," came the voice of Will's father, Professor John Robinson. As was usual after a landing, he ran a backup computer analysis of the planet. "Good old hydrogen-oxygen atmosphere should keep us

3

breathing easy. And the planet seems to have a twenty-seven-hour day. That should give us a few extra hours each day to get the refueling job done. I'm looking at blasting off from here in less than a month."

"Oh, darn," said Mrs. Robinson sarcastically. "You just arrive on a vacation spot and before you know it you have to leave."

Everyone laughed at Mrs. Robinson's joke.

"Some vacation," said Professor Robinson, twirling a finger absent-mindedly on a strand of his lazily trimmed beard. "We'll all be working around the clock. A stop like this is a perfect time to run a ship-wide systems check."

It wasn't very loud, but someone groaned at the idea.

"I know," continued Professor Robinson. "It's no fun, but we haven't checked the *Jupiter 2* from top to bottom since we left Quadrant X a couple of months back. We're overdue. Maureen, you can use the data from this planet to check life sciences."

"Right," agreed Mrs. Robinson. "We can use the data to catalogue the planet as well."

"Judy," Professor Robinson said to his oldest daughter. "In between our duties you can run a physical check-up on each of us." Judy was the mission physician.

"Sure, Dad. I'll go and prepare sickbay," said Judy.

"You might have to spend some extra time checking me out," Major West said to Judy with a typically mischievous grin. He postured his well-cut physique as if he were ready to be examined.

"Look at that," replied Judy smartly as she headed to sickbay. "He hasn't even been out in the sun yet and already he's getting overheated."

"Penny," said Professor Robinson, continuing his orders. "I

want each video-cam and ship monitor recalibrated and white-balanced, okay? Some of the images have been looking pretty psychedelic lately."

"That's because she's been listening to too much of that 1960's rock and roll music from the ship's library," taunted Will.

"What else is there to listen to around here?" shrugged Penny. "It's not like we get to hear any *new* music anymore."

Professor Robinson then turned to Dr. Smith. "Dr. Smith, you and the Robot will help Don and myself with the drilling at the fuel site."

"Robinson," said Dr. Smith. "After all this time you ought to have realized that I'm more suited for guard duty than manual labor."

"I do realize that, Doctor," agreed Professor Robinson. "But the truth is that after all this time I still don't trust you to be alone with my family. So get a hammer and follow us out."

"Very well," said Dr. Smith resentfully. "I'll break out the utility belts."

"And Will —" began Professor Robinson.

"I know," said Will. "Robotics. But, couldn't I go out and explore the planet just a little?"

"That depends on how much work you get done and how quickly you can do it."

"Then I'm getting started right away!" Will replied gleefully.

"Attaboy!" said Professor Robinson.

That was several hours ago. By now Will's diagnostic program was only just starting to slowly run down its checklist. Will realized he would probably never get a chance to explore the new planet.

A series of urgent-sounding beeps interrupted Will's mental

journey. The sound came over one of his computer speakers. It was an alarm that brought the Robotics diagnostic to a dead stop. One of the ship's emergency sensors was picking up signals from somewhere on the planet — something that hadn't been there before.

2
Will Robinson, Explorer

"Dad! Major West!" Will shouted breathlessly as he came running toward the drill site. "There's something else on this planet!"

With the help of their mighty Robot, Professor Robinson and Major West were setting up a five-and-a-half-foot tall laser drilling unit when Will arrived. They had picked one of the few spots that was cleared of the strange huge plants that populated the landscape.

"What are you talking about, Will?" asked Professor Robinson.

"An emergency sensor alarm interrupted my diagnostic array," said Will. "There's definitely something out there."

"We know, Will," said Major West.

"You know?"

"The Robot picked up those readings soon after we cleared this drill site," explained Will's dad.

"My sensors analyzed the new signals as irregular bursts of low-grade electrical energy, Will Robinson," offered the Robot after securing the seven-hundred-pound drilling unit. "At this time they pose no threat to the safety of the crew of the *Jupiter 2*."

"But where do they come from?" asked Will. "And why weren't they there before?"

"There is insufficient data for a complete analysis," replied the Robot. "But it is not uncommon for abnormal environmental patterns to exist on alien worlds that are not yet catalogued in the ship's computer banks."

"Just another example of the danger your father is constantly putting us in, young Robinson," came the voice of Dr. Smith. He had just returned from behind some plants with a sonic recorder in his hands. "For all we know we may already be irradiated beyond human capacity."

"Irradiated?" asked Will with concern. "Dad —?"

"Knock that off, Smith," said Major West. "There's nothing on this planet that can hurt us. But there's something that can hurt you: namely, me, if you haven't finished taking those sonic readings yet."

"I am quite finished, Major," replied Dr. Smith, handing the sonic recorder over to Major West. "Take a look for yourself."

Major West grabbed the sonic recorder and studied it. "Bad news, John," he told Professor Robinson. "Sonic levels are pretty sensitive. If we start drilling we could risk a breach in the planet's subterranean strata."

"That'd cause an earthquake," said Will.

"What did I tell you?" said Dr. Smith. "More danger."

"It's nothing a signal conductor can't handle," said Professor Robinson. "Robot, compute the optimum location for a signal conductor to dampen sonic turbulence."

The Robot paused. "Computation complete," it said, several whirrs and flashing lights of its breastplate later. "Ideal placement for signal conduction would be three miles east of drill site."

"Good," said Professor Robinson as he pulled a palm-sized metallic box out of a supply kit. He handed it to Dr. Smith. "Here you go, Smith. Start walking east."

"Me?" said Dr. Smith indignantly. "Three miles?"

"And when you get there don't forget to flip the 'on' switch," said Major West.

"But isn't it time for lunch?" asked Smith. "I'm famished."

"He's right," said Major West. "Now would be a good time for us to take a break."

"That's the first sensible thing you've said all day, Major," said Dr. Smith.

"I said 'us,' not 'you,'" replied Major West. "You grab a sandwich and start walking."

Dr. Smith was about to protest when Professor Robinson interrupted: "Don's right, Doctor. We really have little time if we want to begin drilling today. I'm afraid you'll have to eat on the way."

"At least let me take a laser pistol for my own protection," said Dr. Smith.

"You're crazy if you let him have a gun," Major West told Professor Robinson.

"Really, Major," said Dr. Smith. "You're becoming more paranoid with each cosmic second."

Professor Robinson pulled out a small laser pistol and holster and handed it to Dr. Smith. "It's a stun gun," he told Dr. Smith. "And it's set low."

"How generous," said Dr. Smith unappreciatively.

"Can I go with him, Dad?" asked Will eagerly. "I'd like to see more of this planet."

"You can't be done with your Robotics diagnostic analysis yet, can you?" asked Will's father.

"All I have to do is restart it," said Will. "It would be hours before I'd have to change its settings."

"I'm afraid not, son," said Professor Robinson. "Your job is to man your station. It's the only way if we're going to survive in space, understand?"

Will nodded. He knew exactly what his father meant. It was something Professor Robinson repeated almost every day. If they were going to survive being lost in space then they had to follow orders.

But no sooner had Will returned to the *Jupiter 2* and restarted the Robotics diagnostic than a thought occurred to him. By simply patching a sub-frequency data chip into one of the ship's portable computers, he would be able to monitor the diagnostic sequence from outside the spaceship. Normally the sub-frequency chips could only work for short-range distances, but Will wondered if he could boost the signal. That way he'd be able to go exploring while manning his station at the same time.

All it would take would be a simple memory download from the *Jupiter*'s mainframe computer banks, Will reasoned as he pulled one of the hand-sized portable computers from a supply shelf in the computer lab. Next, he opened it up. Then, with a small tool the size of an eyebrow tweezer he took one of the tiny frequency chips from their supply box and placed it carefully inside the motherboard of the portable computer. He quickly slipped the portable computer into a specially designed terminal in the lab's main computer and downloaded more memory than was usually used for sub-frequency modems. A few minutes later he was outside the spaceship and turning on the newly souped-up portable computer.

So far, so good. He smiled as he saw that the Robotics diagnostic readings were coming through bright and clear. He walked farther away from the spaceship and saw that the readings still came in strong. Now it was time for the real test. He grabbed a geological knapsack from the ship's utility closet and headed out beyond view of the *Jupiter 2*, constantly referring to the portable computer as he went. He grinned from ear to ear with a sense of accomplishment. No matter how far he roamed from the vicinity of the spaceship, the diagnostic readings continued to come in strong.

Will promised himself to return to the *Jupiter 2* in two hours, just in time to make special adjustments on the diagnostic. In the meantime he began exploring.

The strange plant life on the planet was fascinating, he thought as he examined the mammoth-sized flora closely. It was as though he was looking through a microscope. He could see the fine hairs of a flower petal or the complex veins of a leafy plant with overwhelming detail. Every so often he would cut a snippet from a flower or plant and put it in a special knapsack he brought along. Later, he would run tests on the samples in the ship's lab, hoping to make some exciting discoveries.

The further Will walked, the thicker the foliage around him became. In fact, some of the foliage was so thick Will almost wished he had brought a laser machete to slice his way through it. For the next twenty minutes he continued to explore the jungle-like landscape, constantly checking his compass to make sure he could find his way back to the *Jupiter 2*.

Then he heard a strange sound, a kind of low-grade grumble. The sound startled Will because he knew that there were

11

no animals on the planet and this definitely seemed to be coming from something alive. Whatever it was, it was just ahead of him in a clearing beyond some huge chrysanthemums.

Will braced himself, took a deep breath, then stepped forward to see exactly what lay ahead.

3
Attacked!

"Dr. Smith, wake up!" said Will after reaching the clearing. He had found Dr. Smith snuggled up against some weeds, asleep. The sound he thought was an alien presence was merely the doctor's loud snoring.

Dr. Smith roused himself wearily. His first reaction was to point his stun gun, which lay across his chest for protection. He lowered the gun when he recognized Will.

"Young Robinson," he asked, "what time is it?"

"It's a little after 0-fifteen hundred hours, Dr. Smith," said Will.

"I must have dozed off after that satiating lunch of dried bean curd and vitamin paste," said Dr. Smith with a refreshed yawn.

Will picked up an object from the ground. It was the signal conductor Dr. Smith was supposed to have set-up.

"You forgot to set up the signal conductor," said Will.

"Oh, yes," replied the doctor. "An oversight. I decided to have lunch. I sat down for a moment and must have fallen asleep. I'm sure Major West must be boiling mad since he hasn't picked up the signal yet."

"But you were supposed to head east of the drill site to set up the signal conductor. This is west," observed Will.

"Yes," replied Dr. Smith sheepishly. "I thought I'd take a little detour and enjoy the scenery while I had my lunch — undisturbed, shall we say?"

"Major West isn't going to be happy about that," said Will. "Not when he finds out you deliberately changed direction just so he wouldn't find you taking a lunch break."

"How would he find that out if you don't tell him?" asked Dr. Smith. "After all, young man, aren't you supposed to be back at the spaceship running your Robotics diagnostic?"

Dr. Smith was right and Will knew it. They had caught each other breaking the rules.

"All right, Dr. Smith," said Will. "I won't tell if you won't. But we'd better get this signal conductor set up fast. Without it Dad and Major West won't be able to begin mining for fuel."

"I agree absolutely," said Dr. Smith. "As usual, your command instincts are right on target. After you . . ."

Will looked down at his digital compass and pointed eastward.

"It's that way, Dr. Smith," said Will as he started to lead the way.

"Just a minute, Will," said Dr. Smith. "I forgot my holster."

Dr. Smith had taken off his holster and placed it on top of a nearby rock. He grabbed the holster, but it slipped out of his hand to the ground. But instead of just lying there, it started to sink.

"It's quicksand, Dr. Smith," said Will. "Our planet analysis showed there may be several pools of it in the area."

"Quicksand?" asked Smith. "And I was sleeping right next to it? What if I had turned over in my sleep just a few inches?"

"If we walk slowly and carefully it shouldn't be a problem," said Will. "It's just like avoiding thin patches of ice in a frozen pond."

Will led Dr. Smith away from the quicksand. In a short while the over-sized foliage that had been so characteristic of the new planet began to thin. Eventually there were no plants at all, only vast stretches of desert-like sand and rocks.

"This seems to be the right distance," said Will, coming to a stop. "We can set the signal conductor up on one of these boulders."

"A perfect suggestion," agreed Dr. Smith. "I'll help you up." And with that Dr. Smith cupped his hands together and motioned for Will to start climbing.

"Dr. Smith, this is supposed to be your job," said Will.

"True, William," agreed Dr. Smith. "But it's much safer this way. If you stumbled and fell I could catch you. Could you do the same for me?"

"I guess not," said Will with a grimace. He placed one foot in Dr. Smith's cupped hands and hoisted himself up on a pile of boulders.

"I'll try to reach the highest point," he said as he began climbing. "That should help send the clearest signal possible."

"Good boy," said Dr. Smith. "We'll have that signal conductor set up in no time."

Will felt a sudden rumbling beneath him as he climbed.

"These rocks don't seem very stable, Dr. Smith," he called down.

"Don't worry," said Dr. Smith. "I'm right here to catch you if you should fall."

The rumbling increased. Will felt certain the boulders were beginning to give way.

"This may not be the best location for this signal conductor after all, Dr. Smith," he called out.

Will climbed up a few more feet, then he suddenly stopped and sniffed the air.

"What's the matter?" asked Dr. Smith. "Why did you stop climbing?"

"Dr. Smith," began Will. "Do you smell something strange?"

"Smell something?" asked Dr. Smith, sniffing the air. "I don't think so."

"It smells like sulfur," said Will. He was continuing up the rocks when they suddenly began to rumble again. This time Will froze in his tracks.

"Dr. Smith," began Will. "I'm not certain, but I think there's something behind these rocks."

"Something behind the rocks? Such as what?"

"I don't know," said Will. "But whatever it is, I think it's big!"

Before Will could say another word, a plume of fire shot up from behind the rocks. The flame startled him and he dropped the signal conductor, lost his grip, and went tumbling down the rocks. Fortunately, he landed right on top of Dr. Smith.

"Did you see that?" exclaimed Will.

"I can't see anything," replied Dr. Smith in a muffled voice. "You're sitting on top of me!"

Will rolled off Dr. Smith and helped him to his feet.

"There was a shot of fire from behind those rocks," said Will.

"I'd say you imagined that if your face and hands weren't so suddenly scorched," said Dr. Smith.

Will reached up and touched his face. His skin was stinging with pain. Then he looked down at his hands. They were red with swelling, the kind you get from standing next to intense heat. Will knew he hadn't imagined whatever was behind those rocks. He had a feeling that it was more than just fire and sulfur. In fact, that feeling was confirmed by the sudden sound of a low growl.

16

"What in the world was that?" asked Dr. Smith.

"There's something behind those rocks," said Will. "And I'm going to see what it is."

"Wait," said Dr. Smith. "It's not safe for you to go there. Here. Take my stun laser."

"Thanks for your help, Dr. Smith," said Will, sarcastically. He took the gun. Then he took a step around the rocks.

"Wait, Will," said Dr. Smith. "Give me that gun." Dr. Smith took the gun. "I didn't spend seven years in the millennium wars to be scared off by some rocks. Just make sure your father hears of my bravery." Then he took a deep breath. "Never fear, Smith is here."

Will smiled as Dr. Smith took the lead and began to move around the side of the rocks.

He never even had the chance to peek behind them. Without warning an enormous behemoth leaped out from behind the rocks. Standing well over twenty feet tall it was a dragon-like creature with three heads, two thick arms, and lizard-like skin. Plumes of fire were shooting out of each of its six nostrils. It stood over Will and Dr. Smith and roared as it beat its wide rubbery chest with clawed paws.

"Get back, Will!" shouted Dr. Smith. He aimed his gun at the creature and fired, but the blast had no effect. The creature continued to step forward.

Dr. Smith fired again, this time straight at one of the creature's heads. Still, the creature was not stopped by the blast. Instead it reached down with one of its huge claws and pried the gun from Dr. Smith's hands, sending him tumbling to the ground. It threw down the gun and stepped on it with one of its monstrous feet, crushing the weapon to bits. Then it lifted its foot again and started to bring it down on Dr. Smith.

"Dr. Smith!" exclaimed Will. He grabbed the doctor and

17

started to help him to his feet, but there was little time. The monster's foot was almost upon them.

"Danger! Danger!" came a voice from behind. It was the Robot. It had arrived in the nick of time. It pushed forward, its huge arms fully extended. As soon as it was close enough it let out a series of full-powered laser blasts right at the dragon monster's chest.

Although the blasts did not disable the monster, it startled it just enough to give Will and Dr. Smith a chance to get to their feet and run behind the Robot.

"Robot, am I glad to see you!" said Will.

"I, too, don't mind your interference for a change," commented Dr. Smith.

"How did you know we needed help?" asked Will.

"I didn't, Will Robinson," replied the Robot. "Your father and Major West became concerned when they received no signal from the signal conductor. We have all been searching for Dr. Smith for the last hour."

The dragon monster roared again. Then it let out a series of fire blasts.

"Run!" shouted the Robot. "I will protect you!"

Will and Dr. Smith retreated away from the monster. The Robot extended its arms again and hit the monster with some more laser blasts. But the blasts proved useless against the giant creature. It reached down, scooped the Robot up with one of its hands and lifted it into the air.

"Robot!" shouted Will helplessly. "No!"

The dragon had opened one of its mouths to reveal a set of sharp-fanged teeth glistening with saliva. Will recoiled in horror. The dragon was going to swallow the Robot whole!

18

4
Unexpected Rescuer

"*EEEEEAAAARRRGGGHHHH!*"

Will jumped at the sound of the scream and was relieved to see the dragon monster look away from the Robot. The ugly creature turned its three heads in different directions to see where the scream had come from.

"*EEEEEAAAARRRGGGHHHHH!*" came the ferocious scream again.

Far above the rocks, high in the sky, Will could see something approaching. At first he thought it was a spaceship, but as it drew closer he saw that it was really a kind of hovercraft. It was flat, about three feet wide and five feet deep, and at its bow were a set of handlebars attached to some kind of control panel.

Standing on the approaching glider, one hand on the handlebars and one hand wielding a huge, glowing laser sword, was a boy. A boy, Will noticed, who was probably not much older than himself.

"*EEEEEAAAARRRGGGHHHHH!*" the boy screamed again, this time more fiercely than before.

The boy zoomed earthward, straight toward the dragon

monster, wielding his sword in large, swift circles as he approached. With a swoop of his arm he lopped off one of the heads of the dragon. The startled dragon released its grip on the Robot, sending the mechanical man hurling to the ground.

Almost instantly the Robot's tractor jets kicked in. Instead of hitting the ground full force it landed in an upright position, safe and sound.

"Robot, are you all right?" asked Will with concern.

"I am perfectly all right, Will Robinson," replied the Robot. "But you and Dr. Smith must quickly take cover. I believe we are about to witness a violent battle!"

The Robot was right. By the time it led Will and Dr. Smith to safety behind another pile of rocks, the dragon monster had focused all of its attention on their savior, the boy on the hovercraft. It now was searching the skies with its four remaining eyes, looking for the hovercraft.

The boy was swerving his hovercraft a few hundred feet in the air. Will could see that the boy was preparing to make another pass toward the dragon monster. But Will was concerned. This time the dragon monster would not be taken by surprise. He wondered if the boy could handle the fight alone.

"That boy is no match for that creature despite his skill with that sword," said Dr. Smith, echoing Will's thoughts. "He's sure to be eaten alive."

"Dr. Smith is right, Robot," said Will. "He saved our lives. We've got to do something to help."

"Experience has proven that the creature cannot be harmed by our lasers," said the Robot. "We have little else in the way of weapons. It is my job to protect you and Dr. Smith. Therefore you must stay undercover."

Without effective weapons, Will knew there was little he

could do to help the boy on the hovercraft. He watched as the boy made another beeline toward the dragon monster.

Just as Will thought, the monster was ready for the attack. It faced the approaching boy head on and let out a bright orange shot of fire from one of its remaining mouths. With astute alertness the boy turned the handlebars of his hovercraft and dodged the fiery shot skillfully. Then he swooped down between the dragon's two great necks and, with an expert flick of his wrist, lopped off another one of the heads with his sword. Plumes of blood shot out of the dragon's headless neck, spraying the boy and his craft.

The dragon monster roared with rage, but this did not stop the boy. He drove his sleek glider into the air again and prepared to make what Will hoped would be a final assault. Wielding his sword high above his head, the boy changed direction and headed downward. But this time the dragon monster was too swift. It reached up and grabbed the hovercraft with one claw and the boy with the other. In the confusion, the boy's sword fell free of his hand and disappeared behind some rocks. The dragon monster crushed the hovercraft with one powerful clenching of its fist and tossed it to the ground like a piece of crumpled paper. Then it lifted the boy higher into the air and opened its mouth.

"We've got to do something!" Will shouted with alarm. "The monster's going to eat the boy alive!"

"Save your energy, William," said Dr. Smith. "There's nothing we can do for the boy now. We'd be better off hurrying back to the drill site and warning the others about that monstrous creature. The sooner we get off this planet the better."

Will watched helplessly as the boy, caught in the dragon monster's grip, struggled to break free. Try as he could, he was unable to loose himself. Then Will remembered the boy's sword. It had fallen somewhere behind the rocks on the other side of the dragon monster. Without warning, he ran out into the clearing.

"Will!" shouted Dr. Smith.

"Come back, Will Robinson!" called the Robot.

But by now Will was halfway across the clearing and closing in on the dragon monster fast. The dragon was just about to drop the alien boy into its mouth when Will yelled out:

"Hey, down here! Catch me if you can!"

Upon hearing Will's voice the dragon monster paused. Then it cast its hungry eyes downward. As soon as it spotted Will it reached down with its free hand.

"Run, Will Robinson!" came the voice of the Robot. It quickly shot out from behind the rocks and headed between Will and the dragon monster. "I will protect you!"

Now the dragon monster reached over and made a grab for the Robot. The Robot extended its arm and, instead of defending itself with a laser blast, clamped its sharp metal claws into one of the dragon creature's claws. The dragon screamed with pain.

The distraction gave Will the opportunity he needed. He ran behind the rocks where the sword had fallen. Finding the sword he grabbed it and ran back to the clearing.

"Your sword!" Will shouted to the boy, who was still trapped in the dragon monster's grip. Will threw the sword upward as hard as he could. The boy reached out and caught it. Then he brought it down and sliced clean through the dragon's wrist. The amputated claw and the boy held in it both fell to the ground.

The dragon monster howled in pain as it grabbed its bloody wrist. Freeing himself of the scaly claw, the boy raised his sword and twirled it several times. Then he let it fly straight into the dragon's chest, hitting the monster dead center in what must have been its heart. The dragon clutched its chest, let out one final scream and then collapsed, crashing into the dirt.

In an instant it was dead. Then, in another instant, it took on an electrical glow and disappeared into thin air. Not only that, but all traces of the dragon's amputated parts and splattered blood disappeared as well. Now the only ones left in the clearing were Will, Dr. Smith, the Robot, and the sword-wielding boy.

"Are you all right?" Will asked as he approached the boy.

"I am fine," said the boy breathlessly. He did not look at Will when he spoke.

"That was close," said Will. Then he held out his hand in friendship. "My name is Will Robinson. Thanks for saving us."

The boy ignored Will's outstretched hand. Instead, he suddenly looked straight at Will, rage burning in his eyes.

"I should have let it kill you!" the boy said angrily. "You ruined everything. Everything! I should have let that dragon kill you dead!"

5
Another Attack

For a moment Will was speechless.

"But we helped you defeat the dragon," Will finally replied to the boy, dumbfounded.

"Quite so," added Dr. Smith. "Without us you surely would have been eaten alive by that monstrosity!"

The boy slipped his light sword into a sheath that was attached to his belt.

"That was my Filvid!" the boy said to Will. "And I'm the only Gorpy for this planet. Go find your own planet and your own Filvids."

"What's a Filvid?" asked Will.

The boy laughed at Will. "Good try, Gorpy," he said in an accusing tone. "But you're not going to earn Filvids on my planet. You try that again and I'll kill you."

"I don't understand what you're talking about," replied Will. "What's a Gorpy? What's a Filvid? My family and I are from the planet Earth. We've been lost in space for some time and just landed here to refuel our spaceship, the *Jupiter 2*."

The boy was examining his crumpled hovercraft. "You *are* a

clever Gorpy," he said. "But remember what I said. Find your own Filvids — or die!"

He must have realized his craft was harmed beyond repair. Without saying another word, he slipped behind some rocks and soon was out of sight.

"Charming fellow," said Dr. Smith. "He reminds me of myself when I was a boy."

"Did you understand what he was talking about, Robot?" asked Will.

"Negative, Will Robinson," replied the Robot. "The meanings of the strange words in his language are not in my computer bank."

"You don't need a computer to understand what that boy was saying," said Dr. Smith. "He was quite clear: if we get in his way again he'll destroy us all. It's just as I told your father: as long as we're on this planet we're in danger."

"It sounds to me like it's more a case of mistaken identity, Dr. Smith," said Will. "He was confusing us with somebody else, that's all. I'm sure if we run into him again we can prove we're no threat."

"I suggest we complete setting up the signal conductor Dr. Smith was supposed to install and rejoin the others," said the Robot.

"Good idea," agreed Will. "It should be safe to mount it up on those rocks now."

With the help of the Robot and Dr. Smith, it took less than half an hour for Will to set up the signal conductor. Once they finished, the Robot shouted in alarm.

"Danger! Danger! Aliens approaching!"

"Where?" replied Dr. Smith. "I don't see anything."

"Look at that!" shouted Will, pointing skyward.

Approaching from the horizon were two flying forms. From the distance they looked like birds, but as they came closer, Will saw that they were like no birds he had ever seen before. To begin with, they were huge, the size of a full-grown human adult. And although they had the feathers and wings of hawks, they had heads and arms like giant reptiles. Not only that, but on their heads they wore helmets, the kind a fighter pilot might wear. And in their arms they carried laser rifles.

"They're coming for us!" shouted Dr. Smith with alarm.

But he was wrong. The birdmen were swooping earthward, all right, but they soared right over the signal conductor site and continued onward into the distance. That's when Will noticed what they were really heading for.

"It's that boy," Will said. From his vantage point at the top of the rocks he could see the alien boy who had saved them from the dragon. "He's running across the clearing. The bird-lizards are chasing him! We've got to help!"

"I advise you to stay out of it," Dr. Smith warned Will. "Don't forget that boy's threat."

"But he won't be able to take on those creatures alone," insisted Will. "And if it hadn't been for him we would have been killed by the dragon. Robot, we've got to go down there."

"Negative, Will Robinson," said the Robot, much to Will's surprise. "For once I agree with Dr. Smith —"

"There's hope for you yet," interjected Dr. Smith.

The Robot continued, "We have been warned by the alien boy not to interfere. As intergalactic space travelers we have no choice but to heed that warning."

"But he could be killed —!" insisted Will as he watched the three bird-lizards swoop down on the boy. They began firing their laser rifles at him. The boy, however, was swift on his feet and able to dodge the laser blasts. From his belt holster he pulled his light sword and began swinging it at his attackers. With the first blow he sliced into one bird-lizard's wing. The creature went plummeting earthward. Swiftly, the boy ran to the fallen creature and brought his sword down into its heart, killing it instantly. As soon as this happened the dead bird-lizard took on the same electronic glow that had engulfed the dragon monster when it was killed. Then, just like the dragon monster, the bird-lizard vanished into nothingness.

Will could see the boy breathe a sigh of relief. But before the boy had time to turn around he was swooped up from behind. The second bird-lizard had grabbed him by the collar and was now lifting him in the air.

"It's going to drop him!" said Will. "We've got to do *something*!"

"I repeat, Will Robinson," said the Robot. "There is nothing we can do."

"Hurry, William," said Dr. Smith. "Let us turn on this contraption and return to the others. Perhaps your father will have an idea how we can help the boy."

Will knew that the Robot and Dr. Smith were right. There was nothing they could do except turn on the signal conductor and head back for help.

"I'm inputting the coordinates now," said Will sadly as he pressed a sequence of buttons on the signal conductor. The device immediately came to life with a bright electronic hum that filled the air.

"Let's hurry!" said Will. "We've got to get Dad and Major West to help that boy!"

Suddenly a loud, inhuman shriek stopped Will in his tracks. It was the bird-lizard, who, by now, had lifted the boy hundreds of feet into the air.

"My sensors indicate that the electronic impulse from the

27

signal conductor is causing the bird-lizard great pain," deduced the Robot aloud. "Like many animals it must be sensitive to ultra high-pitched tones."

The Robot must have been right, thought Will. The bird-lizard had raised its claws to its ears as if it were trying to blot out the sound of the signal conductor. Upon doing so, it let go of both its laser rifle and the boy. Then the bird-creature became bright with that familiar electronic glow and vanished into thin air.

"The boy, he's falling!" shouted Will. "He'll be killed!"

Will raced down the side of the rocks and headed across the clearing, but he was too late. The boy had already hit the ground.

6
The New Patient

"He's alive!" said Will upon reaching the boy.

The boy, despite having fallen all that way from the sky, was still breathing. Thinking quickly, Will gently lifted the boy's head with one hand while opening a canteen of water with the other. Will noticed that up close the boy didn't seem as ferocious as he had first appeared. His face was wan and pale, as though he never saw the light of day. His body, covered in brightly colored clothing, was thin.

"Here," Will told the boy. "Drink some of this. You'll be okay."

"Be careful, Will," said Dr. Smith, breathing heavily. "He may be dangerous. Remember his threat."

"Be careful of what, Dr. Smith?" replied Will. "Can't you see he's hurt?"

Will tried again to get the boy to drink some water. The boy responded by pushing the canteen away.

"I don't need your help, Gorpy," said the boy. "I am fine on my own."

"Look, I told you before," said Will. "I don't know who this

Gorpy is. I'm just trying to help you like you helped us. Now drink some water. You need it."

The boy must have been thirsty, because he took a few sips from Will's canteen.

"That's enough," said the boy when he finished swallowing. "You will leave me now. I must continue to collect my Filvids."

The boy started to stand, but found he could not get up. He winced with pain and grabbed his leg. "Owww!" he cried, falling back on the ground.

"Robot, what's wrong with him?" asked Will.

"A scan of the boy's skeletal frame shows some minor fractures to his lower fibula," said the Robot.

"Let me look at him," said Dr. Smith. Dr. Smith gently touched the boy's leg. Upon feeling the doctor's touch the boy winced again.

"The Robot's right," said Dr. Smith. "This boy's leg is in pretty bad shape. He'll need some rest and probably a crutch to walk with."

"I am not hurt!" insisted the boy defiantly. "I am fine! I do not need rest or a crutch! I do not need your help! Go away! Let me alone!"

This time the boy pushed Dr. Smith away and tried to stand up again. But, just as before, he winced with pain and collapsed.

"You're really in bad shape," said Will. He grabbed the boy around the waist and tried to help him up. "We're going to take you back to our spaceship. My sister can have you fixed up in no time."

"No," the boy said, refusing Will's arm. "You're trying to trick me. You just want to steal my Filvids and claim them for yourself. I do not believe my leg is hurt. My Filvid is more powerful than yours. I will make it disappear."

The boy then closed his eyes and concentrated.

"My sensors detect the presence of low-grade electrical impulses," said the Robot. "It is possible they are coming from the boy."

"You mean he's not human?" asked Dr. Smith.

"The boy is humanoid, Dr. Smith," replied the Robot. "But his physiology is definitely alien."

"Robot, are these the same electrical impulses that we detected earlier?" asked Will.

"Affirmative, Will Robinson," replied the Robot. "Not only were these impulses present then and now, but I also recorded their presence when both the dragon monster and the bird-lizard appeared. When they disappeared, the signals weakened and vanished."

"Then this boy is the source of those impulses," concluded Dr. Smith.

"That is a very logical conclusion," said the Robot.

"Thank you," said Dr. Smith.

"That was not a compliment, Dr. Smith," said the Robot. "It was just a statement of fact."

"How *mechanical* of you," replied Dr. Smith, sarcastically, rolling his eyes.

"There," said the boy, opening his eyes. "I am fine now. My Filvid overpowered yours. Now I will be able to walk again."

The boy hoisted himself up with his arms. But once he was upright he winced with pain. It was obvious to Will that his leg was still hurt. Try as he might the boy could not cover up his pain. In a few seconds his leg gave way and he fell back to the ground.

"You see?" asked Will. "You really *are* hurt. Won't you let us help you?"

"It appears I have no choice," said the boy. "But I warn you,

31

Gorpy. I am watching you. At your first attempt to steal my Filvids I will destroy you."

"Whatever," said Will. He had decided to give up trying to convince the alien boy that he meant him no harm. Instead, he ordered the Robot to lift the boy up in its arms. Then, he, the Robot, and Dr. Smith headed back toward the *Jupiter 2*.

"Will, where have you been?" demanded Professor Robinson the moment Will stepped back onto the spaceship. His father, mother, and sisters had already donned their lasers and, together with Major West, had formed a search party.

"Are you all right, Will?" asked Major West. "We were just about to set out to look for you."

"*We* are fine, Major," said Dr. Smith before Will could open his mouth.

Will's mother, Maureen, ran to her son. Her two usually bright eyes were filled with concern.

"Will, we were worried sick about you," she said angrily. "Why did you leave your post?"

"I'm sorry, Mom," replied Will. "I figured out a way to monitor my station and go exploring at the same time — with *this*."

Will showed his mother his specially rigged portable computer. Professor Robinson grabbed the device from Will. Will could see his father was very angry. But before Professor Robinson could reprimand him Judy called out, "Dad, this boy is hurt." She was bent over the alien boy cradled in the Robot's arms. "I'm taking him to sickbay immediately."

Will could see that his parents were surprised to see the wounded alien, but there was little time for explanations. Judy rushed the boy to the *Jupiter 2*'s sickbay and immediately began tending to his leg.

While his sister treated the new patient below deck, Will

told his parents and the others what he and Dr. Smith had seen. He could tell that no one believed him.

"What a bunch of baloney," Penny said with a laugh. Even her alien pet, Blawp, who was wrapped in her arms, let out an uncontrollable guffaw. "You expect us to believe you fought off a twenty-foot fire-breathing space dragon and a couple of flying reptiles and survived to tell about it?"

"But it's true!" insisted Will. "I swear! Dr. Smith, tell them."

"What the boy says is true," said Dr. Smith. "I was there."

"If Smith was involved I'm willing to bet he somehow convinced the boy to make up a fantastic story just so he could explain why he didn't go directly to the signal conductor site," Major West said accusingly.

"For once, Major, your sad attempt to discredit my character will be fruitless," said Dr. Smith with a smug smile. "After all, the Robot was with us. Tell them what happened, Robot."

"Yes," said the Robot. "I can corroborate Will Robinson's story. All he has told you actually happened."

"All right, Will," said Professor Robinson. "I believe you. And, you, too, Dr. Smith. But that still doesn't excuse either of you for not following orders. Now we've lost half a day of fuel production because of —!"

Professor Robinson barely had time to finish his statement when, without warning, a series of the *Jupiter 2*'s alarms began to blast. Next, the ship's lights began to flicker on and off. All around, the instruments on board began to go wild in a seemingly random display of activity.

"What's happening?" asked Penny, clutching Blawp closely.

"My sensors indicate that a high level of random electrical impulses has invaded the ship," announced the Robot.

"Dad! Don!" came Judy's voice over the intercom. "You'd better get down here fast!"

Everyone raced below to sickbay. Once there they froze in awe at the scene. Just as on the upper deck, the sickbay's controls were behaving erratically, most going off their scales. But more shocking than that was the sight of the wounded alien boy. The last anyone knew the boy was lying on Judy's operating table. Now he had somehow levitated several feet into the air and was floating inside a cloudy mass of exploding electrical lightning bolts!

7
The Electric Boy

"I had just given the boy an anesthetic," said Judy. "Then this happened!"

"Any idea what caused it?" Professor Robinson asked.

"Intense electrical impulse concentration is causing instrument mayhem and some environmental turbulence," replied the Robot.

"We've got to get him down from there," said Will, pointing at the floating body.

Major West jumped onto the operating table and reached for the boy. But as soon as he touched the cloudy mass that surrounded the child, a small electrical bolt shot out and hit him, sending him flying off the table and onto the floor.

"Don! Are you all right?" asked Mrs. Robinson as she helped Major West to his feet.

"I feel as though I put my whole hand on a high voltage wire," said Major West. He held his hand in pain.

"Electrical levels surrounding the boy are at two hundred megawatts and rising," announced the Robot.

"Two hundred megawatts!" exclaimed Professor Robinson

with amazement. "But that's enough to power a whole city —
and then some!"

"No human can survive being saturated with so much
power," said Judy. "He'll be killed if we can't get him free of
that power cloud!"

"No *human* can survive it, no . . ." said Dr. Smith warily.
"But who's to say that boy is human?"

"Dad, look!" announced Penny. "Some of these instruments
are leveling off."

Penny was right. The monitors and computers in sickbay
had suddenly started to return to normal. Even the ship's
lights stopped flickering. Seconds later the electrical cloud
surrounding the floating boy seemed to dim. Slowly, the body
began to lower. Soon the cloud had completely disappeared
and the boy lay safe and sound on the operating table.

Judy immediately began checking the boy's life signs.

"Pulse is normal," she said. "And all my instruments show
his body temperature and other vital signs are normal. It's as
if he hadn't been near any electricity at all."

"That's more than I can say for me," said Major West. "My
hand is burning up."

It was true. Major West's hand was red and inflamed from
his attempt to rescue the boy from the energy cloud.

"I'll take care of that," said Judy. She led Major West to a
small box at a lab table and placed his hand inside. Then she
pressed some buttons on the box. The box hummed with activity. When it was over Major West removed his hand.

"It's as good as new," he said with relief. He was now able to
comfortably stretch his fingers. "I'm going to check the instruments upstairs."

"Robot, any idea what caused that electrical turbulence?"
Professor Robinson asked.

36

"Negative," replied the Robot. "Although my sensors have collected certain correlative data."

"Explain," ordered Professor Robinson.

"As at the signal conductor site earlier, my sensors deduced that the electrical impulses detected on this planet seemed to emanate from the boy," explained the Robot. "It is logical to conclude that the same is true now."

"But I am detecting no high-grade electrical energy in this boy's physiognomy," interjected Judy. "He's as normal as any one of us."

"I doubt that strongly," said Dr. Smith.

"More data is needed for a conclusive analysis," said the Robot.

"Well, no matter what, his leg is still in need of repair," said Judy. "And since he's still knocked out from the anesthetic I gave him I'm going to get to work on him."

"John," came Major West's voice over the intercom. "Some of our equipment short-circuited during the turbulence. Another episode like that and we may not be able to get off this planet for months — no matter how much fuel we tap."

"Then we'd better return to the drill site and start digging," said Professor Robinson. "And I want the rest of you to get back to work on your departmental rundowns. Will, this time stick to your post."

"Yes, sir," said Will. "But what about *him*?"

Professor Robinson took a long look at the unconscious young stranger on the operating table.

"Judy, I want you to keep a close check on him while he recuperates," Will heard his father tell his sister. "Once he regains consciousness, we'll find out how he fits into what's been happening on this planet."

Everyone had just begun to disperse when the ship was

suddenly jolted from side to side. Mrs. Robinson and Dr. Smith lost their footing and fell back against a wall. Will and Penny grabbed hold of the Robot while their father held tight to the turbo-lift.

"Robot, what was that?" asked Will after the tremor subsided.

"The planet experienced a subterranean shift," replied the Robot.

"An earthquake!" exclaimed Dr. Smith.

"But there was no sign of substrata instability before we landed," said Professor Robinson.

"The earthquake is a result of the frequent electrical disturbances, particularly that last one," said the Robot.

"John," came Major West's voice over the intercom. This time he sounded frantic. "You better get up here and take a look at this fast!"

Professor Robinson and the others rushed to the upper deck as quickly as the turbo-lift and multi-deck ladders could take them. Once there they found Major West leaning over the seismograph station.

"What is it, Don?" asked Professor Robinson.

"Take a look," said Major West. He stepped aside so Professor Robinson could see the seismograph readings. "Do you know what those readings mean?"

Professor Robinson looked up. He was frowning.

"John, what is it?" asked Maureen nervously.

"The seismograph shows several fault lines near the core of this planet have cracked open," replied Professor Robinson. "Another few tremors like that last one and this planet is liable to blow itself to bits!"

8
The Reluctant
Dinner Guest

Murmurs of dismay escaped the crew as they realized that the planet they were on was not as safe as they had hoped. Dr. Smith pushed through the others and approached Professor Robinson.

"Robinson," he began. "This may sound harsh, but if you want to avoid disaster I suggest you take counteractive measures."

"Oh?" asked Professor Robinson. "What do you suggest, Dr. Smith?"

"That *thing* downstairs," said Dr. Smith. "That boy. Destroy him before he destroys us."

"No!" exclaimed Will, shocked at the idea. "You can't! You can't just kill him!"

"Take it easy, Will," said Mrs. Robinson, placing her calming hands on Will's shoulders. "Nobody is going to harm that boy, Dr. Smith."

"Then you guarantee our destruction, Mrs. Robinson," said Dr. Smith. "The Robot has already told us that the boy is the source of the electrical disturbances. It is the electrical disturbances that have resulted in the shifting of the substrata faults at this planet's core. Any more outbursts by that creature and we're finished."

"You're jumping to conclusions, Smith," said Major West. "The Robot doesn't know conclusively that the alien is responsible."

"Our Robot is merely an overgrown computer drive," Dr. Smith shot back. "In space you have to rely on your human instinct to survive. My instinct tells me that that boy is a threat — and by the expression on your face I can tell that even you know I'm right this time, Major."

"Right or not," Major West replied defiantly, obviously holding back his own brash impulse to jump to conclusions, "if any harm comes to that boy, I'm going to hold you responsible, Smith."

"Do what you will, all of you," said Dr. Smith. "But I am convinced that unless we destroy that alien we won't leave this planet alive."

And with that Dr. Smith walked away abruptly, giving no one the chance to reply.

"Dad," began Will. "Dr. Smith's not right, is he? We don't have to destroy the boy, do we? He saved our lives!"

"Don't worry, son," Will's father replied reassuringly. "No one's going to harm him. After Judy is finished operating on his leg, we'll find out who he is and what he's doing on this planet. Right now we've all got to work really fast to secure as much fuel as possible so we can blast off this planet before there are any more earthquakes."

"Then what are we waiting for?" asked Penny. "I say we get started now!"

"I'm for that!" agreed Will.

The crew quickly returned to their posts and continued running their various systems checks while Professor Robinson and Major West drilled feverishly for fuel. For the remainder of the day there were no more unexpected electrical disturbances nor were there any substrata tremors. By the time evening had arrived everyone was exhausted from their hard work. They collected around the galley table and prepared to eat a well-deserved dinner.

Joining them at the dinner table, under the caring eye of Judy, was the alien boy. Judy had brought him up from sickbay. Sitting in an air-propelled recuperating chair, his bad leg was extended on a plank and encased in a glowing energy cast.

"Hi, there!" Will got up and greeted the boy as he arrived. "Are you feeling any better?"

But the boy threw a stern look at Will and raised his fist. "Stand away or I will kill you, Gorpy!" he threatened Will.

"Excuse me," Mrs. Robinson said to the boy. "You have no reason to be rude to my son."

"Your son?" asked the boy with surprise. He laughed at Will. "You have brought your mother with you to collect Filvids? What kind of a Gorpy are you?"

"There you go again calling me names I don't understand," said Will. "I'll bet it's some kind of an insult!"

"Do those words have some special meaning in your language?" asked Mrs. Robinson.

"That one even sounds like a real mother," the boy said to Will while ignoring Mrs. Robinson's question.

"Look, I don't know what you're talking about," said Will. "That *is* my real mother. And that's my father. And that's Major Don West, our pilot. Over there is my sister Penny and you already know my sister Judy. She's the one who fixed up your leg. Like I told you before, I'm not this Gorpy you keep calling me. We're from Earth and we're lost in space. We just stopped off on this planet to refuel."

The boy threw a suspicious stare around the table. "Oh, I get it," he said. "This whole thing is a Filvid. Perhaps I have misjudged you, Gorpy. Nevertheless, I have warned you. This planet is mine. These Filvids are mine. Do not continue to interfere!"

"This is hopeless!" sighed Will. He returned to his seat at the table.

"I've been having the same problem with him ever since he came to in sickbay," said Judy. "He refuses to believe who we are. He won't even tell me what his name is."

"Great," sighed Penny. "Just what we need around here. Another space *brat*."

"I wouldn't antagonize him, Penny," said Dr. Smith, rising from his seat. "There's no telling what he's capable of. I for one refuse to stay in the same room with him."

With that Dr. Smith took his plate and glass and left the galley.

"Don't let Dr. Smith bother you," Will told the boy. "He's suspicious of everything."

"I am not bothered by any of these tricks," replied the boy.

"You keep calling this a trick," Professor Robinson said to the boy. "Do you mind telling us why?"

The boy did not answer Professor Robinson. Instead his eyes moved hungrily down to the plates of food on the table.

"You're too hungry to answer questions now, aren't you?" Mrs. Robinson asked the boy. "Why don't you come over here and let me serve you some food?"

The boy swallowed and touched his stomach. He was obviously very hungry. He pressed a button on his air-chair console and moved to the table. Mrs. Robinson presented him with a plate of hot food.

"No!" the boy said in a sudden burst of defiance. "I do not need your nourishment! I will survive on my own! I will collect my own Filvids!"

The boy swerved the air-chair away from the dinner table, opened the nearest exit hatch, and flew out of the *Jupiter 2* and out of sight.

9
The Boy From Barakas

"Smile!" said Penny. "You're on *Candid Camera!*"

Penny emerged from the *Jupiter 2* with her portable video camera aimed right at the strange alien boy. Confined to the air-chair, the boy had obviously spent mealtime outside just a few feet away from the spaceship. Upon seeing Penny the boy swiveled his air-chair away.

"Go away," said the boy. "Leave me alone."

"Can't," replied Penny as she followed the boy with her camera's zoom lens. "It's my job to document everything that happens to us while in space. Right now you're more interesting than my father's fuel drill site."

"If only my leg would heal quickly," the boy sighed half aloud.

"What was that?" asked Penny. "Did you say something? Speak louder so my camera mike can pick you up."

"As soon as my leg heals I will continue with my Filvids," the boy told Penny sharply. "Then I will leave this crowded planet."

"That's a good subject to talk about," said Penny. "What is a Filvid, anyway?"

"Why do you and your kind take me for a fool?" replied the boy. "You know perfectly well what a Filvid is."

"Humor me," insisted Penny.

The boy remained silent.

"All right," said Penny. "Well, how about your name. Can't you at least tell me what your name is?"

"I am Movitar of Barakas," replied the boy after a pause.

The Boy From Barakas," said Penny with a smile. "That'll make a great name for this tape. How did you get to this planet? And where do those strange monsters come from? My dad says none of them have been detected on our spaceship's scanners —"

"You might as well forget it," interrupted Will's voice from behind. "He doesn't believe anything we say."

"He's not as tough as he sounds," said Penny, now aiming her camera at her brother as he approached from the spaceship. "I think he's just a little scared."

Movitar swerved around. "Scared?" he said. "Are you calling me a coward? I will prove you wrong!"

"Nobody's calling you anything," replied Will. "But you must admit you haven't been at all friendly to us. And after all, didn't my sister fix your leg?"

"That remains to be seen, Gorpy," said Movitar. "At the moment I am confined to this chair like a prisoner."

"You're not our prisoner," said Will. "You're only in a stasis-controlled recuperating vehicle. You need time for my sister's laser fusions on your leg muscles to set."

"And while I wait you will spend your time stealing my Filvids," replied Movitar. "But I warn you, Gorpy —!"

"Warn me! Warn me!" cried out Will with frustration. "That's all you ever do is warn me! If your leg wasn't sprained I'd take you up on that warning!"

"Oooh, this is good," said Penny, eagerly taping the exchange between her brother and Movitar. "I might even be able to sell this to Hollywood when we get back to Earth."

"Oh, what's the use?" asked Will. "I've got more interesting things to do with my time — like finishing my Robotics systems analyses. And you, too, Penny. You've got plenty of work to do as well."

"I guess so," sighed Penny. "I've been avoiding realigning the ship's sub-space video frequencies. Talk about *boring*!"

Will and Penny returned to the spaceship and resumed their systems analyses. Like everyone else they worked right up until bedtime. The last Will saw of Movitar he was still sitting outside the spaceship pointing. Will could see him through the window as he worked on his Robotics systems check. The boy must have sat out there the whole night because, Will noticed, he was still there the next morning after breakfast.

Will decided to leave Movitar alone. It was clear the boy did not want to be friends and Will did not want to force the issue. But despite the fact that Will had lost interest, Movitar was the subject of discussion when his family gathered for lunch the next day.

"I don't think he's eaten a morsel of food since we took him in," said Mrs. Robinson.

"That concerns me," said Judy, "but his lack of eating hasn't seemed to hinder his recovery. It's almost as if he's used to not eating a lot. It could be a characteristic of his species."

"You mean you got close enough to him to check on his leg?" asked Will. "How'd you get him to let you do that?"

"I didn't have to," replied Judy. "I found him in sickbay when I went to start my systems analyses. He seemed really curious about the medical computers. As soon as he saw me he wanted to run, but not before I had a chance to check on him."

"That's funny," said Penny. "I found him looking over some of my video logs," said Penny. "He seemed fascinated by them. But as soon as I tried talking to him he took off in that air-chair he's laid up in."

"I suspect he's a little more curious about us than he lets on," added Professor Robinson.

"Yeah," said Major West. "John and I saw him watching us from behind some rocks while we were drilling for fuel."

"All this sounds very suspicious to me," said Dr. Smith. "I would not trust him near any of our equipment. He could be a spy."

"A spy for what?" asked Major West.

"We don't know anything about him," replied Dr. Smith. "He could be an advance scout for some alien race. Once they've absorbed our technology they could destroy us, steal our spaceship, and conquer the Earth."

"Yeah," agreed Major West, rolling his eyes sarcastically. "I'd gladly pay them if they could find Earth with our instruments."

Everyone laughed at Major West's joke. Everyone, that is, except Dr. Smith.

"Very funny, Major," said Smith. "Once again your bullheadedness could lead right into the mouth of disaster."

"Smith," said Major West. "I'm wondering if you could shut up for now. You see, I'm trying to digest my food."

Dr. Smith had just opened his mouth to reply when a small tremor shook the ship.

"What was that?" asked Dr. Smith.

"Another substrata tremor?" asked Will.

"Maybe," said Will's father.

"Warning! Warning!" came the Robot's voice over the ship's intercom. It was stationed on the bridge while the family ate.

47

"Electrical impulses detected! Warning! Moderate seismo-graphic readings increasing in intensity."

The ship shook again.

"Don, let's get up to the bridge!" said Professor Robinson. Then he and Major West raced upstairs.

"It's that boy who's causing the trouble!" said Dr. Smith. "If this continues he'll blow this whole planet to bits."

Dr. Smith opened the main hatch.

"Dr. Smith, where are you going?" asked Will with alarm.

"I'm going to do what all of you are afraid of doing," replied Smith as he headed out. "I'm going to destroy that boy!"

10
Monster Petunias and Other Large Flora

"Dr. Smith, no!" shouted Will. "Come back!"

But it was too late. Dr. Smith had already exited the *Jupiter 2*. Will started to follow.

"Will, where are you going?" asked Mrs. Robinson.

"I'm going after Dr. Smith," replied Will. "If he finds Movitar he's going to do something terrible. I know it!"

"Will, I forbid you to go out there," said his mother. "It's too dangerous."

"But Will's right, Mom," said Judy. "Somebody's got to do something. With his leg hurt the boy won't be able to defend himself."

Mrs. Robinson hesitated. "All right," she finally said. "I'll go."

Will beamed a smile of relief as his mother grabbed a laser pistol. But as she headed for the hatch another tremor rocked the spaceship. Mrs. Robinson was thrown hard against a wall. She fell to the floor in a crumpled heap.

"Mom!" shouted Penny as she ran to help her mother. But

Mrs. Robinson didn't move. A cut on her forehead was bleeding profusely. "Judy, she's hurt!"

Judy rushed over with her medical kit.

"She's going to be okay," said Judy as she ministered to her mother.

As soon as Will heard that his mother was going to be all right he looked around and found her laser pistol. Knowing both his sisters were preoccupied with helping his mom, he grabbed the pistol and quietly slipped out of the spaceship.

Once outside, he wondered: *which way?* It didn't take long for him to figure out. Shortly after he reached the overgrown foliage that covered the landscape, Will heard a terrified scream. It was Dr. Smith.

Will aimed his pistol and moved forward through the thick plants and vines. He didn't have to go far.

"Will! Up here!" he heard Dr. Smith call out.

Will stopped at the base of a giant petunia and looked up. It was Dr. Smith, all right. He was trapped in the petals of the petunia, unable to move.

"Dr. Smith, what happened?" asked Will.

"Be careful, Will," warned Dr. Smith. "Don't make any sudden moves. This plant is alive!"

"What do you mean, Dr. Smith?" asked Will. "All plants are alive."

Before Dr. Smith could respond, Will's question was answered. Suddenly one of the vines that hugged the monster petunia reached out and knocked the laser pistol out of Will's hand. Then it scooped Will up, twining itself several times around the boy's small frame. Next, it lifted Will high into the air. Now Will was face to face with Dr. Smith.

"You're right, Dr. Smith!" cried Will. "This plant really *is* alive!"

"No kidding," groaned Dr. Smith at the obviousness of Will's statement.

"But how —?" asked Will.

"The only how I'm concerned about is *how* we can get down from here," said Dr. Smith.

"Will!" Will heard his name called out from below. It was his father. "Will, where are you?"

"Dad! Up here!" Will called out. Below he could see that his father, armed with a laser rifle, had come searching for him.

Professor Robinson looked up. When he saw Will and Dr. Smith in the grip of the monster-sized petunia, he raised his rifle and aimed at the plant. Before he had a chance to pull the trigger, something grabbed him around the legs. It yanked him to the ground, forcing him to drop his rifle. Next, it began pulling Professor Robinson toward a muddy pool of quicksand.

"Dad! Look out!" shouted Will from above. "It's quicksand!"

But try as he might, Professor Robinson was unable to break free of the powerful vine that had trapped him.

"This is our fate, then," said Dr. Smith. "To die as plant food . . ."

"No one's going to die, Dr. Smith," said Will. "Not if I can help it!"

Will placed his hands together and began hitting the petunia vine that bound him, but it was useless. His blows didn't phase the monster flora.

"What's the use, Will?" asked Dr. Smith. "Can't you see this time it's truly the end of us all?"

"EAAAARRRRGGGGGHHHHHH!!!" came a scream from above. Will recognized the scream instantly. He had heard it once before — the first time Movitar had rescued him from the three-headed dragon.

"EAAAARRRRGGGGGHHHHHH!!!" came the scream

51

again. Will looked up. It *was* Movitar. He was swooping down in his air-chair, his light sword raised high.

Then, with one fell swoop, Movitar swerved between Will and Dr. Smith and cut them free from the plant. Will and Dr. Smith fell, unharmed, to the ground. The petunia turned on Movitar, lashing out at him with giant, finger-like strands. The boy was almost as skillful at avoiding capture in the air-chair as he had been in his hovercraft, Will noticed. He sliced away at the attacking vines. After a moment, the entire petunia exploded in a bright electrical glow and disappeared.

"Dad!" cried Will, his attention now focused on the plight of his father. He raced over, grabbed his father's hands and tried pulling him out of the quicksand, but the pull of the muddy pond was too strong.

"Dr. Smith!" Will called. "Help us!"

Dr. Smith looked around for a weapon, but found none. Instead, he ran over and began pulling on Will in the hopes that four hands would work better than two.

"It's hopeless, Will," said Dr. Smith as he realized the pull of the quicksand was too great. "Your father is finished! We have to save ourselves!"

Dr. Smith let go of Will and ran off, back toward the *Jupiter 2*.

"Dr. Smith!" Will called out in a panic. "Come back! I'm not strong enough to do this alone!"

"Will!" said Professor Robinson. "Go back to the ship! There's nothing you can do!"

"No, Dad!" said Will as he struggled to pull his father free of the quicksand. "I won't leave you! I won't!"

"EEEEAAAARRRRGGGHHHHHH!" screamed Movitar from above. Seconds later the alien boy swooped down in his air-chair and pulled Professor Robinson out of the quicksand. Then he moved Will and his father to dry land.

"Thank you," Professor Robinson told Movitar. "We owe you our lives."

"You owe me nothing!" Movitar replied in his usual brusque tone of voice. "Once again you have interfered with my —"

But Movitar was unable to finish his sentence. He winced with pain and reached for his wounded leg. Then his eyes rolled back into his head and he passed out.

11
The Dare

Will was standing right beside Movitar when he came to in sickbay almost an hour later.

"He should be all right," said Judy, who had just finished freshening Movitar's stasis cast. "The combination of the excitement and his stasis cast was just too much for him." Then she said to the boy, "Still, it's not all bad news. Despite your stubbornness your leg is strong enough for you to walk on. In the future, you should listen to your doctor when she tells you to rest and recuperate."

"I listen to nobody," replied Movitar defiantly. "I am capable of surviving on my own."

"Tough guy," quipped Judy. Then she began putting her medical equipment away.

"How do you feel?" Will asked Movitar.

Movitar looked away and would not answer.

"Look, why don't you knock it off?" Will said, finally losing his patience. "You're not so tough. Otherwise, why would you save me and my dad from the quicksand? You even saved Dr. Smith and he doesn't like you."

"I do not need anyone's affection," said Movitar. "I can survive on my own without anybody. Unlike you . . ."

"What do you mean unlike me?" asked Will. "I've been doing pretty well since we've been lost in space. I once had to rescue my family from a planet run entirely by robots. Then there was the time my sister Penny and I were trapped inside an asteroid in Quadrant X. Have you ever been attacked by an army of rock men —?"

"Rock men?" laughed Movitar. "Don't make me laugh. I have trained in the Pits of Barakas. My father is a great warrior who will one day be proud when I have collected all my Filvids. He is not like your father, who needs to be rescued by his own son from a pool of dirty water!"

Will was angered by Movitar's statement. "Watch what you say about my dad," he shot back. "He's braver than anyone I know."

"Ha!" laughed the boy. "Your father is a weakling. Why, he nearly got the two of you killed."

"You better take that back or I'll —!" started Will.

"Boys, what's going on here?" asked Judy when she returned.

"He's calling Dad bad names!" said Will.

"I merely state the truth," replied Movitar.

"Now stop this, both of you," said Judy. "If the two of you can't be friends then I suggest you spend as much time away from each other as possible."

"That'd be my pleasure," said Will.

"I have no desire to befriend anyone from your planet," said Movitar, seeming to agree.

"My planet?" asked Will. "Wait a minute . . . are you saying you now believe who we are? That we're from Earth?"

"I have had time to study you," said Movitar. "I have come to the conclusion that what you have told me is the truth."

"Then you no longer think I'm this *Gorpy* you kept calling me, whoever that is?"

Movitar laughed. "Your brainpower is as weak as your physical strength, human," he said. "A Gorpy is not a *who*, it is a *what*. In fact, I myself am a Gorpy."

"Huh?"

"A Gorpy is someone under the age of twelve of your Earth years who undertakes the Barakan Ritual of Dangers," explained Movitar. "I am such a person."

"You mean that dragon and those bird-lizards were part of some kind of test?"

"You call them tests," replied Movitar. "We call them Filvids. Yes, the destruction of those creatures helped to prove my worthiness to become a Barakan warrior like my father. The same goes for those monster plants I rescued you from."

"But where is your father?" asked Judy. "We know there were no other people on this planet until you arrived."

"Barakas is far away," answered Movitar. "It is in the solar system of the G'bor sun. When it is time for a Gorpy to pass through the Ritual of Dangers he is sent to the most hostile world in the known universe. He is left there for the rise of seven suns —"

"That's about a week on Earth," said Will.

"During that time the Gorpy must survive horrifying danger," continued Movitar. "Often he will not know what that danger is or when it will appear. When the last sun has risen, if the Gorpy is still alive, he has officially become a warrior."

"You mean your parents just leave you here alone?" asked Judy with concern.

"I am well armed with my light sword," said Movitar. "The

same light sword my father used when he was a Gorpy at my age. The same one used by his father and his father before him. My family is the most feared and respected of the warrior families on Barakas. We are the strongest in the universe!"

"Well, you won't be strong at all unless you postpone your adventures and let your leg heal," said Judy. "Do I have your word you'll do that?"

"I will neither agree nor disagree with your request," said Movitar. "It is I who will decide when I will leave."

"I wish I could talk with your parents right now," said Judy with obvious frustration. "I would make sure they kept you in bed."

"My parents would laugh at your medicine," said Movitar.

"You are a simply infuriating child," said Judy. Then she returned to her business of checking her medical systems.

"What are you doing?" Movitar asked Will. Will had pulled out his portable computer.

"I'm just checking the systems analyses I'm running on my Robotics station," replied Will. "I linked this portable computer up so I could monitor my station from afar. Want to see?"

"Scientists!" laughed Movitar upon seeing the computer. "On my planet the scientists are the weakest of all the people. We warriors do not need robots and computers in order to survive in space."

"I doubt that you could fly a spaceship without a computer," said Will.

"On my world you must learn to survive with your wits alone," replied Movitar. "You would not survive a single day on Barakas. You could never be a warrior."

"I can survive pretty well on my own," said Will. "Before we took off from Earth my sister and I spent an entire summer at space camp! You're not the only one who has been trained in survival techniques."

"Ha," laughed Movitar. "Survival techniques. After several hours in the wild I am certain you would be crying for your Robot."

"How much do you want to bet?" asked Will.

"A wager is worthless since you would not survive to pay the debt," said Movitar.

"You name the time and place," said Will.

"Very well, human," said Movitar. "This evening, after your family has gone to bed — meet me at the clearing beyond the giant plants. I dare you to see who is the better warrior."

"Wait a minute, what about your leg? My sister will be pretty angry if you go out tonight."

"Just as I thought," said Movitar. "You'll find any excuse not to face my Filvids."

Will glanced around to make sure his sister was out of earshot.

"It's a deal!" he told Movitar.

12
Escape From
the *Jupiter 2*

Later that evening Will made certain that no one would suspect he planned to leave the spaceship. He gathered with his family at the dinner table, as usual. Then he proceeded with his evening chore: the writing of his daily Robotics diagnostic summary and submitting it to his father for approval. Finally, he played a leisurely game of holographic chess with Dr. Smith and the Robot and went to bed.

Being the youngest, Will was the first to sleep every night. This night, however, he stayed up in his cabin until he was certain that the rest of his family had turned in. Then he slipped back into his clothes and sneaked out.

He got as far as the main hatch when he saw Movitar standing face-to-face with the Robot.

"Your Robot refuses to allow me to leave the ship," said Movitar upon seeing Will.

"He's just doing his job," said Will. "He's supposed to protect members of the crew while we're asleep."

"I am neither a member of your crew nor am I in need of protection," said Movitar.

"He doesn't know that," replied Will. "To him you're just a friendly visitor."

"He thinks I'm your *friend*?"

"Yeah, go figure," said Will. "The Robot is programmed to recognize non-hostile aliens."

"Your Robot is wrong," insisted Movitar. "I am a powerful foe. I am to be feared."

"That's what you say," said Will with a shrug. "But the Robot doesn't seem to agree, do you, Robot?"

"My sensors do not detect a dangerous presence at this moment, Will Robinson," replied the Robot. "However, the presence of both of you here at this hour does not compute. It is far beyond your bedtime."

"We've got some important business outside, Robot," said Will.

"My computer banks do not contain special instructions that allow you to leave the spaceship at this hour, Will Robinson," replied the Robot.

Will glanced, red-faced, at Movitar. The alien was giggling at him. Will was embarrassed.

"Robot, I *order* you to let us out," insisted Will.

"I am not programmed to obey that order," replied the Robot. "Such an order can only come from Professor Robinson or Dr. Robinson."

"Some spaceman," Movitar said, laughing at Will. "It seems you are the servant of your Robot!"

Will opened his mouth to reply, but before he could say anything the hatch door slid open and his father walked into the spaceship from the outside, a small piece of drill-site equipment in his hand.

"Will," said Professor Robinson with surprise. "What are you doing up this late?"

"Dad —!" said Will in reply. "I thought you were asleep . . ."

"Obviously," said Professor Robinson. "What you didn't know was that I decided to double check this condenser unit before I turned in. So answer the question: what's going on?"

"Your son claims he is not afraid to face the Barakan Ritual of Dangers without the aid of your Robot or your technology," said Movitar. "I doubted him strongly, so I challenged him to join me as I collect the rest of my Filvids. However, no sooner had we tried to leave the spaceship than the Robot protected him like he was some helpless pet."

"I am not a pet!" exclaimed Will. "The Robot was just under orders to —"

"That's enough," Professor Robinson said sternly. "Neither one of you should be up this late. Will, you have a full day of work ahead of you tomorrow. And, Movitar, you're not leaving here until your leg is completely healed."

"But, Dad," started Will. "You don't understand —!"

"I don't need to understand anything," replied Will's father. "Except that your behavior is rash and very irresponsible."

"But, Dad," said Will. "He called you names —!"

"I don't care what he did," Professor Robinson said, interrupting his son. "I forbid you to leave this spaceship. Now, I want both of you to get back to bed. We'll all have a long talk about this in the morning."

Will returned to his cabin, but try as he might, he could not fall asleep, not with thoughts of what Movitar must be thinking of him swimming in his head. He was certain that his failed attempt to meet Movitar's dare had convinced the alien boy of one thing: that Will's father *was* weak and Will himself unable to survive without the protection of the Robot.

What's more, Will was convinced that his own father didn't believe that he could meet Movitar's challenge. It was a thought that troubled him deeply.

For a long time Will sat at his desk and stared absent-mindedly at the items there. There was his cabin computer, his holo-music-video chamber, his personal tool kit. There was even the palm-sized portable computer he rigged to run his diagnostic program. These were all the things he loved and cherished. They were the things that made him feel like he was alive.

But Movitar had made him feel like he couldn't survive without these things. Was the alien boy right? Up until now Will had not given it much thought. What if something happened to the spaceship and he and his family were forced to survive with no equipment at all? Worse yet, what if something then happened to his family and Will was left all alone to fend for himself on some alien planet? Could he do it? he wondered.

He had to prove Movitar wrong! But how? *How?*

The answer, he realized, was right in the palm of his hand. He had picked up the portable computer while his thoughts had been wandering. Now his mind focused on the small object in his hand. It was the solution he was looking for.

Within minutes he raced to sickbay. By then, Movitar had fallen asleep. Will shook him until he woke up.

"What is it you want, human?" asked Movitar, quite disturbed to be rustled from sleep. "I was dreaming of the glory I will achieve upon my return to Barakas."

"Come with me," said Will. "We're getting out of here."

"Don't make me laugh," said Movitar. "You can't even breathe around here without permission."

"That's where you're wrong," said Will. "I know a way we can get out of here right now."

"Oh, yeah? And what about your Robot?"

Will held his chest out defiantly. "I'll have the Robot under control in no time," he said. "With *this*." He held up his portable computer.

"Explain yourself," demanded Movitar.

"Come with me and see for yourself," said Will.

Will led Movitar to the main deck, but the two boys remained behind an archway that connected the turbolift area to the helm where the Robot was stationed.

"The Robot is about fifteen feet away from my Robotics station," explained Will as he began adjusting the controls on his portable computer. "I rigged this portable computer so I can monitor my station from various distances. However, not only can I monitor it, I can control it, too. Right now I'm creating a sub-program that is designed to cause a major conflict with the systems running at my station. The Robot is linked to my station by means of a special remote frequency. In case of a malfunction he is designed to physically link himself to my station and use his main drive to keep the Robotics systems on the ship running. The Robotics systems' own backup systems are supposed to kick in before the Robot is ever needed to interfere, but the way I'm arranging it, each backup system will shut down before it has a chance to respond. Watch."

Will proved himself right. It took only a few seconds after he punched some entries into his portable computer for an alarm to go off at the Robotics station. Almost instantly the Robot moved to the station. A compartment panel at its waist opened. Then it pulled out a multi-pin cord from the compartment and plugged it directly into a socket at the station. As soon as this was done the alarm stopped.

"Done," said Will.

"That's it?" asked Movitar. "Your description of it took more time than the actual doing of it."

"The miracle of modern science," replied Will.

"But what's to stop the Robot from preventing us from leaving?"

"What I did was create a Ground Zero emergency shutdown of the Robotics systems," explained Will. "At Ground Zero all previous orders programmed into the Robot are canceled out so he can put all his efforts into keeping the ship running. We're free to leave anytime we want."

Will stepped out from behind the archway.

"Let's go," he said, leading Movitar out of the spaceship.

13
Terror From the Depths
of the World

"I hope you are this clever when we face real danger," said Movitar as he and Will made their way through the over-sized plant life. "Your portable computer will prove useless against my Filvids."

"You've got to admit you wouldn't be able to collect any more of your Filvids tonight if it wasn't for my 'technology,'" said Will.

"It was *your* way," said Movitar defiantly. "I would have thought of another way to get out of your spaceship."

"You've always got an answer for everything, don't you?" asked Will.

"A good warrior knows the answer before the question is asked."

"Oh, yeah?" asked Will. "Then what am I doing now?" Will had stopped and was once again adjusting the controls on his portable computer.

"If you were smart you would be returning the power to the Robotics stations and returning your Robot to his post," guessed Movitar. "That way no one will know for several hours that we are gone."

"That's a pretty good guess," said Will. It was exactly what he was doing. "I'm impressed."

"It was obvious what you were doing," said Movitar.

"You know, you could make a pretty good scientist — if you ever wanted to, that is," said Will.

Movitar stepped toward Will. "You will not call me that!" Movitar said angrily. "I am a warrior, not a scientist." Then he grabbed the portable computer out of Will's hand, threw it on the ground, and crushed it with his feet.

"Hey!" said Will, picking up the shattered device. "What did you do that for?"

"Enough talk," said Movitar. "We do not need your device for what we are about to do. It is time for you to see what real danger is like. Let's go."

They walked for nearly an hour. Movitar, limping on his weak leg, led the way. They had gone far beyond the giant plants. They had even gone beyond the rocky signal conductor site where Will and Dr. Smith had first encountered Movitar during the fight with the three-headed dragon and the lizard-birds.

Along the way Movitar seemed to have some slight trouble walking, since his leg was still healing.

"Are you all right?" asked Will. "Do you want to rest?"

"I do not need rest," said Movitar. "I am accustomed to surviving with pain. I would not be surprised if it was you who needed rest."

"I can go as long as you," said Will. "Even longer."

"We shall see about that," said Movitar.

They continued on. Soon after they started Will began to sense a change in the cool night air.

"I'm beginning to feel warm," he said. "How about a water break?"

"Yes," said Movitar. "Water. But we must not drink too much. First rule of survival in the wilderness is to conserve rations."

The boys stopped and opened their canteens. After taking a sip of water Movitar said, "One sip is enough for me now."

"Me, too," said Will, putting away his canteen. "But, man, it's really getting hot. And the sun hasn't even come up."

It was true. Will was sweating from top to bottom, almost as if he were in the middle of a hot Arabian desert.

"This doesn't make any sense," said Will. "The Robot catalogued this planet as Type Three. Temperature modulations are only supposed to range within five to ten degrees in its complete four-hundred-and-ninety-three day year."

"Just another example of how being dependent on your computers could cost you your life on an unknown planet," said Movitar. He, too, was drenched with sweat.

"Man, I sure could use another drink of water," said Will through parched lips.

"To drink water now is to give in to weakness, human," said Movitar. "Drink if you must, but I will not."

Will grabbed his canteen, desperately wanting to crack open its cap and drink the refreshment inside, but he held himself back from doing so.

"No," he said. "I can make it without the water."

"A brave choice, I must admit," said Movitar.

Will smiled. It was the first time Movitar had said anything positive to him.

A second later Will's smile gave way to a startled frown. The ground beneath him was beginning to tremor.

"A tremor," said Will. "The substrata faults must be moving again!"

"Does that frighten you, human?" asked Movitar.

"It concerns me," replied Will. "Major West said these earthquakes could result in this entire planet blowing up. What good would your Filvids do you then?"

"I am not afraid of the consequences," said Movitar. "Run back to your spaceship if you're so scared."

Again, Will was tempted to do what Movitar said, but held his ground instead.

"No," he said. "I'm staying!"

All at once Will felt the earth beneath his feet heave with such a force that both he and Movitar were thrown to the ground. Before they could get back up the earth broke open in front of them. Huge plumes of fire shot out from somewhere inside the planet.

"That fire!" shouted Will over the din of the shaking earth and the roaring flame. "That must be the source of this great heat!"

"More than that," said Movitar. He struggled to his feet and pulled out his light sword. "It is my new Filvid!"

No sooner had he said the words than an enormous figure climbed out of the fiery crack in the ground. Will could tell at once that the figure was humanoid. It had a head, two arms, and two legs. At over twelve feet tall the creature stood like a man, but unlike a man it was covered from head to toe in scorching hot red and yellow flames.

"Behold, human!" shouted Movitar to Will as he raised his sword at the fire-man defiantly. "A Fire Dweller of Barakas!"

14
The Superior Warrior

"Movitar, what are you going to do?" asked Will frantically. "I will destroy him," replied Movitar as he moved toward the fire-man, wielding his light sword high above his head. He charged forward, but just as he did the fiery monster reached down and grabbed the light sword right out of his hand, melting it upon contact. Then it reached down again, this time trying to grab Movitar.

Movitar stumbled back, but his weakened leg made it hard for him to run far. He fell to the ground. The fire-man closed in quickly.

"Movitar!" shouted Will fearfully. "What's wrong?"

"My leg is too weak," replied Movitar. "I cannot run!"

Will ran to the boy, grabbed him under the shoulders and dragged him away from the horrible attacker. He pulled Movitar as hard as he could, stopping when he reached the safety of a tree.

"Maybe it won't see us here," said Will. His hope was short-lived. Will saw the tree jolt. Within seconds it was being pulled right out of the ground and lifted into the air by the fire-man.

Will and Movitar looked up at the monster helplessly. The

tree itself was now aflame and before long had been reduced to nothing more than a burned cinder.

"We are helpless, human," said Movitar. "The fire-men do not use their eyes. They go by touch and sound and destroy anything and everything in their paths. Because of my leg I cannot outrun it, but you have a chance to flee."

"No," said Will. "I won't leave without you."

"Don't be a fool," said Movitar. "You will be destroyed."

The fire-man tossed the remains of the tree away. One of the cinders, Will noticed, hit the ground and sank. It landed right in a pool of muddy quicksand.

"That quicksand," pointed Will. "It may be our only chance."

"What are we supposed to do?" asked Movitar. "Jump under the sand and hold our breath until the monster goes away? We wouldn't survive that."

"True, but I have an idea." Will stood up and walked as close to the fire-man as he could without getting scorched.

"Hey, you!" Will shouted up. "Fire guy! Down here!"

The fire-man looked around, searching for Will.

"Don't be a fool, human!" warned Movitar. "You'll be killed."

"Not if I can help it," said Will. "Back on Earth we have a saying: 'survival of the fittest.' Right now I'm hoping for 'survival of the *smartest*'!"

Will continue to egg on the fire-man.

"Hey, dumb-head," Will called out. "Down here!"

The fire-man looked down and spotted Will. Now it moved menacingly forward. Will stepped back.

"Let's go," said Will, helping Movitar to his feet. Then he led the boy to the far side of the pool of quicksand.

"Hey!" Will shouted up at the fire-man. "Here we are."

The fire-man spotted Will and Movitar and began to make a beeline toward them, but the boys did not run.

70

"I think I know what you're planning," said Movitar. "But if it doesn't work it's the end of us!"

"Then let's hope it works!" said Will. "Hey, fire-man, over here!"

"Yeah, over here!" Movitar called out.

Will and Movitar watched as the fire-man followed the sound of their voices. The only thing between them was the pool of quicksand. With its inability to see the quicksand the fire-man's foot sank into it with its next step. The pull of the quicksand was great. Try as it might the fire-man was unable to break free.

"It's working!" said Will. "YEAAAH!"

The fire-man was sinking. First his legs disappeared, then his torso, then his arms. Soon his head sank under the weight of the heavy sand. In the end there was nothing left except a thin stream of smoke that rose out of the quicksand itself.

"We did it, Movitar!" exclaimed Will happily. "We did it!"

"No," said Movitar. His voice sounded upset and angry. "It is not right. I am the warrior, not you. I am the stronger."

"What difference does it make if we're safe?" asked Will. "Helping each other is the best way to survive. That's how it is in my family."

Saying so made Will remember how often his father had told him the same thing. He wondered what his father would think of him now. Instead of following his father's orders and doing his part to help his family he had gone out on his own to prove he could survive. But was that what survival was really about? he wondered.

"I am not a part of your weak family," Movitar replied interrupting Will's thought. "I will not be helped!"

At those words there was another rumble from beneath the ground.

71

"Another earthquake," said Will.

But it was more than an earthquake. A hand reached out from the pool of quicksand. It was a black, burned hand. The hand grasped the solid ground that surrounded the pool of quicksand, then pulled its body out. It was the fire-man — or what was left of it. A burned, black mass of charred flesh.

"I don't get it," said Will, shocked. "Nothing can survive that quicksand!"

"It is *my* Filvid," said Movitar. "*I* will be the one to collect it, not you!"

The charred fire-monster inched its way slowly toward the children. The ground began to shake even more violently. Will and Movitar fell down. Within seconds the monster was hovering over them. Will closed his eyes and screamed as the creature reached down to grab them. He braced himself for the worst.

But it never came. All of a sudden the ground stopped shaking. Will thought he sensed a sudden bright light when his eyes were closed. When he opened them the charred fire-monster was gone. In its spot stood Movitar.

"It's — gone," Will said with amazement. "But how —?"

"It was my bravery," said Movitar proudly. "I destroyed the monster."

"But with what?" asked Will. "We don't have any weapons."

"If you were not cowering you would have seen how a true warrior destroys his enemies," said Movitar. "I guess this proves who is the superior warrior."

"I guess so." Will sighed, defeated.

"Will! Movitar!" The boys heard someone calling them from above. They looked up. Professor Robinson was descending from the sky, a jet pack strapped to his back.

"Uh-oh," said Will. "It's my Dad. And he looks angry. *Very* angry."

15
The Truth About Filvids

"**W**ill, there is absolutely no excuse for what you did!" scolded Professor Robinson after he escorted Will and Movitar back to the *Jupiter 2*.

Movitar had been taken to sickbay immediately and Judy was now checking over his leg. Will was planted in a chair in the galley and forced to confront his mother and father.

"Your father and I are both very disappointed in you," said Mrs. Robinson. "Do you know what kind of danger you put us all in?"

Will knew. It was the earth tremors that woke everybody up, explained his parents. No one knew if the planet would survive this new round of tremors. His father and Major West considered an emergency blast-off. That's when Penny noticed that Will was missing.

"Why, Will?" asked Professor Robinson. "Why did you deliberately ignore my orders?"

"I wouldn't have done it, Dad, except —" Will started.

"Except what, son?"

"Movitar said that you and I were weak," explained Will. "That we couldn't survive without help."

Professor Robinson paused and glanced at Will's mom. Will could tell immediately that his father was not the least bit disturbed by the accusation. Instead, his father dropped to one knee and looked Will squarely in the face.

"Is that why you're doing this, Will?" he asked. "Because of what Movitar thinks of us?"

"But we're not weak, Dad," said Will in reply. "You're the strongest guy I know!"

"And you're the bravest son I know," said Professor Robinson. "And as long as we both know these things that's all that really matters. To me, anyway. Maybe on Movitar's planet they have a different idea of how fathers and sons should be. But I think we've done pretty well by each other lately. You know that when you're in trouble, or confused, or even a little scared, you can come to me to help figure things out, don't you? Just like I know you'll be right there when I need you. Haven't you learned by now that the only way all of us are going to survive in space is by working together?"

"I know that, Dad," said Will. "I thought of it when I was alone with Movitar outside. I even told him we had to help each other. I guess you're right. I guess they do things differently on his planet."

Will knew that he was probably going to be punished severely for his actions and he was ready for the consequence. But just when he thought his parents were going to tell him the punishment, Major West appeared with the Robot by his side.

"John, I know I'm interrupting," said Major West. "But I've got some startling new data about these earth tremors."

"What is it, Don?" asked Professor Robinson.

"The Robot has a theory that is almost impossible to believe."

74

Will knew the news must be important for Major West to interrupt a private family discussion. Luckily for him, his punishment would have to wait.

"Go ahead," Will's father told Major West.

"Tell them what you told me, Robot," Major West ordered the Robot.

"I have completed my analysis of the frequent electrical impulses we have been experiencing on this planet," began the Robot. "The source of them is Movitar, the boy from Barakas."

"We know that, Robot," said Mrs. Robinson.

"It is the electrical impulses that are responsible for the sub-strata disturbances that threaten this planet," the Robot added.

"Are you positive?" said Professor Robinson.

"I have triple-checked my findings, Professor Robinson," replied the Robot.

"There's more, John," said Major West. "Tell them the rest, Robot."

"I have computed that other than Movitar there are no other life forms on this planet," continued the Robot.

"That's true," said Mrs. Robinson. "We checked that out before we landed here."

"I am speaking specifically of the appearances of the strange life forms that attacked Movitar, Will, and Dr. Smith while they were outside," said the Robot. "The three-headed dragon, the bird-lizard, and the fire-creature."

"The Robot makes a good point, John," said Major West. "Why is it our ship's instruments have never picked up those monsters as life forms?"

"Can you explain that, Robot?" asked Professor Robinson.

"My analysis shows that the life forms are comprised completely of electrical energy," answered the Robot. "The same kind that has created an imbalance in the planet's sub-strata."

"You mean those monsters weren't really alive?" asked Will. If it was true he couldn't believe it, not when he could still feel the scorching hot effects of the fire-man on his skin.

"Negative, Will Robinson," replied the Robot. "At the moment you encountered them they existed, but not as a bona-fide life form."

"You're not making any sense, Robot," said Mrs. Robinson, somewhat impatiently.

"The creatures Will encountered are an extension of the electrical impulses generated by the alien boy," said the Robot.

"Don't you see?" asked Major West. "What the Robot is saying is that Movitar creates these things out of thin air. Somehow he manufactures them with his thoughts. Then, when he's done with them he makes them disappear."

"But what about the Ritual of Dangers?" asked Will. "If those creatures don't really exist, then —"

"Then Movitar was never really in any danger," concluded Major West. "He was always able to *think* those things away."

"That's how he destroyed the fire-creature," Will said, thinking back. "That's how he got it to climb out of the quicksand and attack us. When I closed my eyes he made it disappear. Then he lied to me. He told me he destroyed it. All so he would look like the superior warrior."

"Not only that, but every time he thinks one of these things into reality he creates such an intense electrical force that it further upsets the natural stability of the environment around him," said Major West. "Remember the electrical cloud we saw when we first brought him to sickbay? Judy knocked him out with an anesthetic to operate on his leg. The Robot thinks that his subconscious took over and created a burst of electrical power."

"It's not true!" came a voice. Everyone turned to see Movitar standing there. It was clear that he had overheard most of what Major West and the Robot had told them.

"It's not true!" he insisted again. "I am not making my Filvids up!"

A moment later Judy appeared behind the boy. "I was trying to check on his leg and he just took off."

"I do not need your medicine," said Movitar. "And I am not making my Filvids up! I am going to be a great warrior like my father!"

Mrs. Robinson stepped toward Movitar. "It's all right, Movitar," she said sympathetically. "We understand. Children on our planet also like to make up games to play with imaginary characters. There's nothing wrong —"

"It is not imaginary!" insisted Movitar. "It is real! I will show you! I will face the greatest danger yet! After this there will be no doubt of my bravery!"

"Movitar, wait —!" started Will.

But it was too late. Movitar ran out of the spaceship and disappeared through the forest outside.

For a long moment Will stared through the viewport.

"Will, are you all right?" asked his mother.

"I guess so, Mom," said Will. "Movitar has got to prove that he can be a grown-up in his own way. I guess my way is different. And right now my way is to help get this ship in top working order so we can leave this planet safely and find our way back home. Right, Dad?"

Will saw a smile come over his father's face.

"Right, son," said Professor Robinson proudly. Before he could say any more the ship shook violently. The jolt was so great the entire deck seemed to heave at a deep angle.

"That was the biggest one yet!" said Major West as he regained his footing and checked the seismograph. "Watch out! Here comes another!"

Another quake jolted the ship.

"We're being knocked off our landing legs!" said Major West.

"Warning! Warning!" said the Robot. "Seismographic activity is increasing. Fault lines near the planet's core are in danger of being breached. Recommend immediate evacuation of planet!"

"The Robot's right," said Professor Robinson, looking at his instruments. "We've got less than half an hour before this planet blows itself to bits!"

16
The Dark Search

"*C*an we blast off, John?" asked Mrs. Robinson. "Do we have enough fuel?"

"Barely," replied Professor Robinson. "But it's not blasting off that I'm concerned about."

"I know what you're concerned about, Robinson," said Dr. Smith. "We may be able to get back up into space all right, but once there, how long can we fly?"

"Smith's right," said Major West. "In fact, I don't even know if we have enough fuel to pull out of this planet's gravitational force. And if we *can* pull out, the chances are slim that we'll have enough fuel to get us to another habitable planet."

"We'll have to try, nonetheless," said the Professor. "I'd rather take our chances in space. Together we may be able to do it. Agreed?"

Everyone nodded in support.

"But what about Movitar, Dad?" asked Penny. "According to Will his hovercraft was destroyed by the dragon monster. How is he going to get off the planet?"

"Maybe he doesn't have to," said Will. "Maybe none of us do."

"What do you mean, son?" asked Professor Robinson.

"Movitar is the one causing the earthquakes," explained Will. "If I can find him, maybe I can get him to stop."

Will was right and it was obvious his father knew it. "According to the instruments we have less than thirty minutes before the sub-strata faults at the core of this planet become breached," his father told him. "After that, there's no telling how soon the planet might explode."

"He can't have gotten too far," said Will. "If we can find him I know I can talk him out of what he's doing — for now, anyway."

"If Will can buy us some time so that we can ration some more fuel, I say we try it," interjected Major West.

"All right, Will," said Professor Robinson in agreement. "You and I will take some jet packs and look for Movitar. But we've only got twenty minutes. After that we get back to the ship and blast off."

"Roger, Dad!" Will agreed eagerly. He hurried to the supply closet and pulled out some jet packs. From the corner of his eye, he saw his father take Major West aside for a private conversation. He didn't have to guess what the conversation was about. He knew that his father was telling the ship's pilot that if he and Will didn't return after twenty minutes the crew should blast off without them. Will pushed the terrifying thought to the back of his mind and concentrated on the task at hand. He knew finding Movitar would be easy. The hard part would be convincing him to stop his Filvids long enough to give the Robinsons a chance to escape.

By now it was morning, but the sky was dark with clouds of black ash spewed from some nearby volcanoes. The constant rumblings from within the planet had set them off.

"Will, do you see any sign of Movitar yet?" Professor Robinson shouted across the sky after he and Will had been jetting through the air for a few minutes.

"Nothing yet, Dad," Will called back. The black clouds were making it difficult for Will and his father to see as they jetted through the air in search of Movitar. In another few minutes Will was having trouble even seeing his father.

"Dad? Where are you?" Will called out. "Can you hear me?"

"I can hear you, but I can't see you," replied his father. Professor Robinson's voice sounded dim, as if it were receding into the distance.

"Dad!" called Will. "Dad!"

But Professor Robinson did not reply. Then it hit Will: He and his father had been separated in the blinding darkness. To make matters worse, Will could no longer see the ground below. His sense of direction was thrown off. Was he flying straight ahead or backward? Was he flying up or down? He couldn't tell.

"EEEAAARRRGGGH!" He heard the cry from somewhere below. It was Movitar!

"Movitar!" shouted Will. "Can you hear me?"

"EEEAAAAARRRGGGH!" came the cry again.

Will angled the controls on his jet pack downward as best as he could. Movitar's warrior cry was clearly coming from below. Will used his ears and moved in the direction of the cries. Soon he was able to make out an opening at the top of a hill. No, it wasn't a hill, he realized. It was the mouth of a volcano. And Movitar was inside it!

Will lowered himself into the stony opening. Below he saw a figure moving about. It was Movitar, all right, but he wasn't alone. The three-headed dragon, the bird-lizards, and the fire-man had all somehow come back to life. They had cornered Movitar inside the mouth of the volcano cavern and were closing in on him fast!

17
Like Father, Unlike Son

Will swooped down into the mouth of the volcano. Movitar was trying to flee the attacking monsters. But Will could see there was no place for him to run.

"Climb on, Movitar!" called Will as he lowered himself between Movitar and the monsters.

"No," Movitar shouted at Will. "Stay away! I do not need your help!"

Will looked at his watch. Time was running out. "But you've got to stop what you're doing, Movitar," said Will. "If you don't, you'll blow us all up!"

"That's a lie," replied Movitar, one eye on Will and the other on the creatures.

"It's true," insisted Will. "These dangers are all in your mind. You can make them go away if you want to. And when you do the earthquakes will stop!"

"I will prove to you that I am a great warrior," said Movitar. "I will destroy these creatures. I will!"

"Don't you get it, Movitar?" asked Will. "You can't prove how brave you are against something that isn't real."

"They are real!" cried Movitar. "They are!"

"All right," said Will. "Let's see how brave you are. Why don't you go ahead and destroy them already? The sooner you do, the sooner we can get out of here."

"I will!" insisted Movitar. "I will! You watch me."

Movitar looked around and then grabbed some fist-sized rocks. He threw the rocks at the marauding monsters, but the creatures were not stopped. Then one by one the monsters began to close in.

"No," Movitar said to the monsters, his arms raised in fear. "Go away! Go away! Why won't you go away?"

"You can't get rid of them this time, can you?" asked Will. "Why?"

"I do not know!" said Movitar.

Suddenly the rumbling beneath them became stronger.

"This volcano," said Will as he felt the tremors increased. "It's going to blow! Climb on, Movitar. We've got to get out now!"

Movitar nodded and grabbed Will around the shoulders.

"Hurry, Will," said Movitar pointing to the monsters. "They're getting closer!"

Will switched on his jet pack. Then nothing.

"What's wrong?" asked Movitar.

"I don't know," said Will. "It won't go on. But it doesn't make sense. I checked it before I left. It was full of fuel."

Will and Movitar were trapped. Unable to fly away they cowered against the cavern wall as the monsters slowly approached them.

At that very moment the earth tremors suddenly stopped. A sudden calm took over the ground. Then, one by one, the three-headed dragon, the bird-lizards, and the fire-man generated a brief electrical glow and disappeared into thin air.

"They're gone!" said Movitar. "And the earthquake. It's over, too. Look, the sun is coming through!"

Will looked up at the mouth of the volcano. A bright, blinding light was now coming through the opening, but it wasn't the sun. It was a small spaceship lowering itself into the volcano.

When the spaceship landed, two adults emerged. One was a man, one was a woman.

"Mom! Dad!" said Movitar with a big smile. He ran to the two new arrivals.

"We have found you at last, Movitar," said the man who must have been Movitar's father.

"Are you all right, son?" asked Movitar's mother.

"Yes," said Movitar. "I am fine. Father, I have survived the Ritual of Dangers! Now I am a true warrior!"

"Is that so?" asked his father with a suspicious tone of voice.

"Yes," replied Movitar. "At last, I am a warrior like you."

"But what about that last danger, my son?" asked Movitar's father. "It seemed that both you and this alien boy were about to be destroyed."

"I would have destroyed those creatures had it not been for the weak human, Father," insisted Movitar. "He interfered."

"That's not true!" said Will, stepping forward. "I was trying to help you. You almost wiped out my entire family!"

"Father, don't believe him," said Movitar. "He was never really in any danger."

"But I do believe him, my son," said Movitar's father. "Because what Will Robinson of Earth says is the truth."

"You know my name?" asked Will with surprise.

"Yes," replied Movitar's mother. "We know everything about you and your family. We have been watching on our monitors ever since we pinpointed Movitar's location."

"We tried to get here as quickly as we could," continued Movitar's father. "But Movitar had run quite far from home."

"I did not run away!" insisted Movitars. "It was time for me to face the Ritual of Dangers!"

"Run away?" asked Will. "I don't understand."

"You see," continued Movitar's mother. "Thousands of Earth years ago we were a violent warrior race. It was common practice for young children to battle monsters to prove their worthiness."

"But today a small, influential group of Barakans are more interested in science than in warfare," added Movitar's father. "Most of the planets in our galaxy have begun to live in peace. Over time my people have finally realized that the battles we must fight are not against strangers from other planets or other solar systems, but against the common enemies of disease and famine. For the first time in my planet's history the scientists are being listened to. I myself am in charge of my entire planet's scientific movement."

"You mean, you're kind of like a president of scientists?" asked Will.

"In a way," came the answer.

"Then you're not a great warrior, like Movitar said?" said Will.

"Is that what my son told you?" asked Movitar's father.

"Yes, sir," replied Will. "He said he was trying to be a great warrior like his father, that you had sent him here to prove himself."

"Nothing could be farther from the truth," said Movitar's father. "However, I suppose I can't blame him for making up that story. You see, Will, most people on Barakas are still warriors. They are still clinging to the traditional ways. And many Barakan children still pass through the Ritual of Dangers in order to prove themselves to their parents."

"The other children in Movitar's school would often make fun of him for being the son of scientists and not warriors," said Movitar's mother. "Recently, after just such an incident, Movitar was so ashamed he ran away. We've been looking for him ever since."

"The other kids will not make fun of me now!" declared Movitar. "I survived the dangers!"

"You survived nothing except your own thoughts," Movitar's mother told his son. "When we saw the danger you were putting Will and his family in we stopped your ability to create monsters with the power of *our* thoughts."

"How can you do that?" asked Will.

"Our brain waves are closely tied to the natural electrical currents of nature," explained Movitar's mother. "On our world the frequency between our thoughts and nature are balanced. We can't make our thoughts a reality. But on this planet our thoughts are stronger than nature. This is something that Movitar did not know when he first arrived here. When he found there were no real monsters here he created them out of his mind."

"You mean all this was to prove something to your dad, Movitar?" asked Will.

It was clear that Movitar could no longer hide the truth. He turned away. "My father does not understand, Will," he said quietly. "The other kids make fun of me. They do not like me. They go on great hunts with their fathers. All my father wants to do is conduct scientific experiments. He has no time for me. Not like yours does for you."

"But my dad gets pretty busy, too, Movitar," said Will. "There's lots of times when it seems like he doesn't have time for me either. Before we took off from Earth I hardly knew the guy existed."

"That can't be true," said Movitar. "He risked his life to save you in the plant forest. And you said that you help each other to survive in space."

"We've learned a lot about how we *feel* about each other since we've been lost in space. I guess you could say being in this fix together has made us kind of understand each other more."

"The same can be true for us, son," Movitar's father said, kneeling down. "In my desire to help our people change, I didn't realize how little attention I've been giving you. From now on it's going to be different. I've already made plans to cut my schedule to be with you more, lots more. And guess what? As soon as we get back, you and I are going on a survival expedition. Just like the other kids."

A big smile came over Movitar's face. "Really?" he asked. "Just you and me?"

"Yes, son. You see, just like Will's father needs *his* son's help, I need *your* help, too."

"I can help you?"

"Yes," said Movitar's dad. "You can help me to become a better father."

Movitar seemed to understand exactly what his father meant. A tear rolled out of his eyes as he rushed into his father's arms.

Just then the sound of a jet pack was heard from above. It was Professor Robinson lowering himself into the volcano pit. Will ran to his father and gave him a warm hug. Then he introduced his father to Movitar's parents and explained everything.

"I'm sorry for all the trouble I caused, Professor Robinson," Movitar told Will's father. "But that's over now. The planet is safe and you can continue to mine for fuel."

"Good-bye, Movitar," said Professor Robinson. "And good luck."

"Good-bye, Movitar," said Will as Movitar and his parents prepared to leave in their spaceship.

"Good-bye, Will," said Movitar. "And thanks."

"Thanks? For what?"

"For helping me learn that proving myself to my father is easy. You just have to start by understanding each other. I hope you and your dad find your way home someday."

"We will," replied Will. He felt the touch of his father's hand on his shoulder. "As long as we keep searching *together.*"

Will climbed into his father's waiting arms. Then Professor Robinson switched on his jet pack, and father and son took off out of the mouth of the volcano and headed toward the *Jupiter 2.*